THE MOJAVE ROAD
AND OTHER JOURNEYS

For J. Christ
and Larry

Bruce Williams
2011

THE MOJAVE ROAD
AND OTHER JOURNEYS

POEMS BY
BRUCE WILLIAMS

TEBOT BACH • HUNTINGTON BEACH • CALIFORNIA • 2010

Cover image and author photo: Grace Corcoran
Design, layout: Tania Baban-Natal, Conflux Press

ISBN 13: 978-1-893670-50-1
ISBN 10: 1-893670-50-3

Library of Congress Control Number: 2010926100

A Tebot Bach book

Tebot Bach, Welsh for little teapot, is A Nonprofit Public Benefit Corporation which sponsors workshops, forums, lectures, and publications. Tebot Bach books are distributed by Small Press Distribution, Armadillo and Ingram.

The Tebot Bach Mission: Advancing Literacy, Strengthening Community, and transforming life experiences with the power of poetry through readings, workshops, and publications.

This book is made possible by a grant from **The San Diego Foundation Steven R. and Lera B. Smith Fund** at the recommendation of Lera Smith.

www.tebotbach.org

For Ellen Williams

and for Casey, Drew, Beth,
Kathleen and Grace

TABLE OF CONTENTS

III: THE MOJAVE ROAD AT LAST

THE JOURNEY OF BRUCE WILLIAMS

The prophets and the poets have traditionally looked to the desert to find revelation, clarity, and direction in their lives, both spiritual and otherwise. Yet, in their wanderings, we have no doubt that they considered not only the materials and events of their lives but also those conditions of their own mortality—and the precarious claim to mortality of all sentient life—that arose to the forefront of their meditations. In the literature of seekers, the vision sought after might be otherworldly, yet it invariably reflected directly upon the life of the seeker himself. And the seeker returned to his community, his tribe, his family, his apostles, to recount the experience of that journey.

Bruce Williams' *The Mojave Road and Other Journeys* is simply one of the most breathtaking and heartbreaking collections of poetry I've read in many years. These poems constitute a sequence of elegies and a folio of meditations upon illness, death and transcendence, and also upon the nature of late, redeeming love. As in Theodore Roethke's psychologically dense, timeless, and powerful poem, "Journey to the Interior," Bruce Williams' spiritual self-confrontation charts a dangerous, often precarious landscape of intimate loss and the consequent potential for the wreckage of the self.

There is a fierce courage in these poems, and the same clear-eyed regard of the world we admire in the poetry of Jack Gilbert. In the constellation of metaphor, if death is the "tenor" of these poems, then certainly Bruce Williams' Jeep is the "vehicle" that delivers him not only into the arid center of the desert but also safely back out again into this world. In Bruce Williams' Inferno, his Jeep serves as both his Virgil and his Beatrice as well. Some journeys relish their endings, those celebrations of the homecoming; some journeys regret the empty stillness after travel. The best journeys remain those, which, like this extraordinary volume of poems, will seemingly always continue.

—David St. John

I:
GETTING IT FIXED

GETTING IT FIXED

The clerk in oncology discovers your wife is
a divorce lawyer. Says: That must be depressing
work. A speaker blares: code red, rear lot.
A hundred and six outside. Small lesions
rupture. Systems break completely. From
the window you see two men in green scrubs
sprinting with metal canisters toward a yellow Jeep,
blazing between a blue Lexus and a black Aerostar.
More shouting, bursts of foam. We all watch.
The Jeep will need reconstruction, but damage
doesn't spread. Finally the clerk remembers
to schedule the appointment with the surgeon. You think
of a joke. Don't say your wife does spousectomies—
write the time down in a surprisingly neat hand.

REPAIR

He's tired of all the cancer poems leaked from
that new fountain pen. Increasingly he lives inside
his Jeep—the car guy he never was before. He drives

north through Barstow. Las Vegas drags traffic toward
State Line. But he unhooks for Afton Canyon, follows
the dirt road down to where the Mojave River stays

a river all year round. Not the Grand Canyon
of the Mojave, as guide books say, but a deep slash
where pack trains and Model T's paused for water and rest,

often stayed stopped by sand and mud. The place
Ron, who had taught him four-wheeling, bogged down
his Blazer just a month ago. Now he walks the crossings,

cold, muddy water swirling an inch above his knees.
Then drives carefully, following old tracks, keeping on
the high side of each hole. After the third crossing

he relaxes. But avoiding a boulder, he backs across broken
tamarisk into his first off-road flat—what he feared for months.
Why he bought that huge off-road jack he could barely lift

and left in his garage. He uses the small jack included with the car.
Hot day—ATV brats blast by, ignoring him. Sand. He slips
a board beneath the jack, a trick he read about, stands

on the tire iron, bounces since the lug nuts are too tight
for his arms. Late afternoon. At night he's almost blind.
That's when the snakes will swivel out. He does what he must,

one lug nut at a time. He mounts the full-sized spare he strangely
remembered to inflate. He torques it on—the canyon's red
a deeper sunset red. When his doctor called after the checkup

he was sure it was to scold about too many eggs. He was surprised when Ron got stuck here. He re-negotiates the water, not walking now. He reaches the crowded highway. Wasn't hard at all.

Afton Canyon, March 2004

AFTER VISITING HIS UROLOGIST,
HE THINKS OF THE MOJAVE ROAD

Near the top of the list of what he wants to live
not read about, if he has time. Now almost 130

miles, 124 unpaved, longer when it was the trail,
Jedediah Smith moccasined toward what he'd

never seen: Mexican soldiers, San Gabriel adobe
walls, the San Joaquin before it was the San

Joaquin—thick with marshes, deer and Tule elk.
Still long, in 1925 when Bill Robertson,

hired gun for the Ox Ranch, and Matt Burts,
ex-hired gun, shot each other for a radiator

full of water at Government Holes—
last cowboy killing over water rights.

Too long in 1949 when an off-course
blizzard sealed homesteaders in twelve-foot

drifts that filled Black Canyon Road until
there was no road or Black Canyon anymore.

Scat of history: burro, camel, rusted fence
and mine, intaglios, petroglyphs, names

and dates from Rock Creek's scurvied soldiers
trying to graffiti their way back home,

dry water tank with "Ox Ranch" fading from
the side. Beautiful—somehow in ways

I'll have to say, then scratch at rock and plant
to show: sandstone, granite, lava, jasper, silver,

borax, agate, talc—creosote, palo verde,
ocotillo, yucca, smoke tree, mesquite,

Joshua, tamarisk, palm. Lanfair Valley,
Afton Canyon's fluted, high rock walls,

and Soda Lake—white as a blank page, almost
as dry, crusted salt and sand, but lately

four inches down water, quicksand muck.
Last person to make it across in three months

a Ranger. Foolish as accepting a drunken pass,
she slammed her truck in four-wheel compound low,

  sliding and slipping, gunned it all the way, her white
  truck brown to the headlights. Over the phone she says

"I never want to do anything like that again."
He tells her, "I never want to try," but asks if

she'd lowered the air pressure in her tires. "No."
Stars multiplied, track of coyote, snake, sunrise

slapping empty land. Who knows what will happen
next? You gather information like kindling, rocks.

for Dick Barnes

DISCUSSING THE MOJAVE ROAD WITH ODYSSEUS

I say I'm glad he's coming along.
My wife can't be with us either.
And there won't be much water,
only a trickle in Afton Canyon,
none, I hope, across "dry" Soda Lake.
He's happy Jeeps once carried warriors.
He'll bring a skin of wine, bread, cheese,
no maps because there's Athena,
two long, sharp spears and a bronze sword
with a jeweled handle. The spears
might help with snakes. But my Jeep is plain
as a hand-built raft. We could sell the sword,
buy air lockers, a six-inch lift, alloy wheels,
thirty-five-inch Mud Swamper tires
and a winch to help us through
sand and muck. Unlike my poet friends,
the ancient man knows about such things.
All good gear. But he'll keep the sword.
He feels its edge. If we get in trouble,
out there, he's sure there will be other Jeeps.

ALLUSION: MARCH 21, 2003

Maybe it will all work out:
a clone of us
or Texas
tethered in the East

well-fed smiles
gleaming
like a limousine,
peace, smooth as oil.

But
remember the end
of *the Odyssey.*

After the Trickster killed
everyone
who made him mad

they wiped the blood
from the tables
and hung the serving girls.

But fathers
and brothers reached
for their own spears.

Then Athena
shot down from Olympus
to staunch the feud
for the liar she adored.

Think
of a desert
crushed tanks
broken cities
vultures

fathers, mothers, sisters

no Athena there.

"FIGHTING CANCER"

Maybe those words are wrong and can lead to a burnt Bruce policy,
the siege of my colon, bladder, kidneys—the retreat from the body's
Moscow or a last stand in the Alamo or Little Big Horn of the brain.
So I ask: Could we just get along, have some kind of truce, agree to
co-exist? I want to ride my Jeep down dirt roads, watch the mountains'
purple turn to red. See my teenager become someone I don't almost
hate. Help my wife negotiate with a relative of yours. Add a few more
anniversaries to our stack. And you, sweet cancer, love your creativ-
ity, your experiments with cellular revision, your variations on normal
cells' dull themes.

I say, you can keep the prostate, or at least most of it, and plant your
slow gardens. But stay there. I admire your energy, ambition, your
desire to feed the earth. But be satisfied. No new outposts on the body's
West Bank, dismantle any there, and I'll send no suicide-chemo in.
Let's be friends. Live together until a new enemy appears.

LESSONS

His doctor wanted the boy to be
one of them. The boy refused because
of blood. The same with hunting.
He didn't love deer but couldn't
open what he might kill. Even fish
inside their scales had too much blood.
But now the hospice nurse teaches him
to clean and bandage his wife's cancer
wounds. Ellen calls him Nurse Bruce.
They talk of how she'll be a playful
ghost for him: a pinch or kiss when
he's with his new loves—a leprechaun
sized Ellen, scanning the living room,
riding the luggage rack of their Jeep.
He's careful as he works, changing
the dressing daily, watching what
he could never watch. The trick,
as always, is to blot, not scrub, with
soft white gauze, switch gloves every
step, never break half-formed scabs.

COMPENSATION

Cancer thins her
to a hotter flame.
Every other week she buys
new clothes. People
compliment until they
look close, and she tells
them, "You don't want my diet."
Each morning he holds her
keeping off the cold.

May 24, 2006

AFTON CANYON AGAIN

North of Barstow. Where the Mojave road
climbs out of sand to desert water soaking
through the heat. Where the wagons filled
their barrels, after dry Soda Lake, and arrows
cutting stragglers down. A few deep
holes to drink from and navigate. Where
Ron and Maria almost drowned their Blazer,
and I crossed, then sliced a tire and fixed
the flat in twilight and deep sand. Three times
there, but I've never made it to the end.
But a winter's rain can change everything.
I call the Barstow B.L.M. The Ranger says
he drove the canyon about a week ago.
The usual crossings weren't too bad, but keep
away from the rest of the river bed. Too much rain,
quicksand there. Stay on the road near
the railroad tracks and be careful of the spot
where everything except a thin path
is washed away, drop-offs on both sides.
He had a friend get out and guide him there
so the Explorer wouldn't slide off the edge.
Ellen is through with a round of chemo,
and we drive out, drop our bags in a motel
and make the canyon in the afternoon.
Thinking of the West Nile Virus and eroded
immunity, I give her a long sleeve shirt,
smear repellent on her face and arms.
The Ranger's right. The water crossings
are shallow silted in by winter floods.
The rest of the riverbed a gooey trap. By
next winter they plan to wash Ellen's
bone marrow out and try to fill her up
from someone else. We reach the dangerous
drop-off spot, cross quickly, looking
to neither side. Then we look for "the Caves,"
where travelers rested and sometimes hid.

Intaglios near them on the mesa. Pictures
flat, not carved on the canyon side.
Can't find either place. Turn around.
Pick up our bags. Drive home.

FAIRY TALE

Ellen likes the story poems best, and so do I. There was an old
man and old woman who lived on a hill. They watched the sun
strike the buildings down below, the mountains rub their snow
against the sky. They listened to the wind clearing its hot throat,
the rain splashing off their slanted roof. Then they left. Birds
swept off the junipers and ash, snakes crawled from under the
prickly pear, skunks flashed their ribbons of black and white,
raccoons dropped half-washed food. Everyone howled and hissed
and sang. And then they all went away.

JORDAN

They take the Jeep to Jordan,
seven miles north of Lee Vining, off
the new power plant road. Pavement,
then a damp, muddy track. Jordan,
the old power plant, nearer the mountains.
February 7, 1911. Snow, twenty-two
feet deep. The town a few people,
tending the new electricity. Night.
The whole side of Copper Mountain
slides down. Lights in Bodie dim.
A rancher on snowshoes discovers
the avalanche. Bodie is balcony deep
in twenty-eight feet of snow. Rescuers
come on skis. Fifty-five below.
A woman and a dog survive. Now
Jordan's a few concrete foundations
and blackened cans and pipes. Past
the ruins, the road curves. Up
a slope. a small graveyard, the markers
white stone. All dead the same
day, except for one unfortunate
alive until the eighth. The woman
lost a leg. Frozen ground. Bodies
waiting in an unheated shed for
spring and burial. The whole Owens
Valley came. Now hardly anyone
in Lee Vining, even at the Save the
Lake Foundation, knows of Jordan.
The road turns east through tall grass,
blackbirds, a small stream. We descend
toward the sheen of Mono Lake.

A GIFT

Last day. Hospice.
She tells the children
she loves them.
Tells me thank you
after I say she's
beautiful. Then
gurgles and jerks.
Morphine by schedule,
but she could have
more if I want.
How can you know
if someone half
comatose has too
much pain? Then
I realize why it's up
to me and what more
morphine could mean.
I call the doctor.
How can I choose?
He tells me he'll take
that choice away
from me: doubles
the regular dose.
Two hours. We're
all there, touching her,
wiping up blood
oozing from her nose
and mouth. She takes
a ragged breath. Stops.
Fools us. Takes one
more. She's gone.

Sunday, September 24, 2006
9 p.m.

II:
RECONSTRUCTION

AFTER HE BRINGS HER ASHES HOME

Ellen sits
on the mantle,
seared inside
her cedar box.
There and
not there
            like him.

October, 2006

RECONSTRUCTION

We sat on the terrace outside the taverna. The real
Delphi a mile down the road around a bend—
excavated walls, a theatre, temples, a stadium. This
was the new Delphi where archaeologists moved
the village some sixty years ago, when they began to dig.
Wasps landed near our food, attracted by local
drinks: carbonated lemon, orange, cherry juice
sweeter than Seven-Up or Coke. George trapped them
under a glass, blew cigarette smoke inside and watched
them writhe. His friend, Allen, back from the hospital,
drank wine and laughed. Women and George love Allen
less frequently. Now Allen's dark, handsome face was lined.
But only by a burst appendix. George blew more smoke.
The wasps inhaled the vapors, but didn't prophesy.
The disease was miles south and years away.
Nothing seemed symbolic. Yellow flowers grew
next to marble on the hillsides. It was spring.

for G.H., Delphi, 1966

INNOVATION

The Buick had a broad smile
and a green back.
It would take them
in its soft belly carefully
and they would go to the park
to feed the ducks
or outside of town to the place
where airplanes liked to fly.
In the backyard was the incinerator
with its hot smell and red mouth.
He was careful there.
Then they sent the Buick away
for a blue, tight-lipped Ford.
He didn't cry. He felt afraid.

Denver, 1949

TO BE REVISED YEARLY

For Ellen

December 20, 1996

Almost solstice.
Ten years ago
our old house burned.
You rushed
into my arms.

Fire has made
and unmade my life.

Like you.

STILL SMALL VOICE

Like a fat man crammed in a cheap suit
real problems are never encompassed
by anticipation. As when a hypochondriac
feels small teeth gnawing at his stomach
then reads his wife's biopsy report.
Or the way my house burned from
a short-circuit curling through the walls,
not the dry brush igniting on the hills.
Or how when my daughter reached
thirteen, I was certain fights would
flash over a plunging short dress,
tattoos, piercings, condoms sliding
from her purse. But find my daughter
campaigning for a bullhorn this Christmas—
a bullhorn that carries three football
fields, and includes a siren as well.
Perfect for the picket line, or a church
youth retreat she plans to lead.
No bullhorns says her Dad. *Why not?*
This house is a bullhorn free zone.
All right, forget the present.
She'll earn her own money baby-sitting
No bullhorns yells fascist Dad *Not
even if you baby-sit a thousand years.*
Besides who needs a bullhorn the way
that you both shout says Mom.
But Mom thinks—*maybe when
the daughter's late for school
on the phone or draining all
the shower's heat, when he's lost
in another half-funny poem,
or when they're both downstairs
and I'm upstairs in bed
and ache too much to move. . .*

San Dimas, 1997

35

HOMILY

Above the oldest Colorado town
Christ in bronze twists through
twelve stations of suffering. But
down from the shrine, the valley
green, then blue toward Taos.
North of us Mt. Blanca a jagged
cup of Navajo-sacred snow. This
should be enough. Then a snake
speeding behind my bare legs.
Looping down, cutting towards
the next switch-back in the path.
Just a gopher snake. Still heavy,
longer than the rattler I almost
stepped on at our cabin. Dark
marked, a bluish tinge. Muscle
of persuasion. Scroll of fear.

San Luis, Colorado, July 1998

PERSPECTIVE

I loved Kit Carson
when I was a boy
because he was small
and brave

before I knew
the scent
of burning fruit
heard of Canyon de Chelly—

when the Navajo were
the rugs
on Grandfather's floor,
the silver on his hand.

STRATIFICATION

North of Taos the Rio Grande cuts its gorge.
Claudia showed me the bottom thirty years ago
when we stayed at the Lawrence Ranch. A surprise.
A few miles off only a shadow—an eyebrow—
penciled line. Close, dark rock walls opening.
We followed a dirt road. Then an old horse path
to hot springs beside the river—both extremes.
In the damp heat, a second couple. Hesitant,
embarrassed. Claudia thought it was the marks,
webbed scratches, across her skin. Now I try
many small roads. Give up. Turn back.
Afraid of tires spinning deep in sand. From a bridge
on the highway tourists can look down. My wife and I
stop with the others. I walk across. Walls darker,
higher than I thought—rock brutality: below
the green-string river: a motionless diorama, reconstructed
past. Later at the ranch, I'm told Claudia's settled
on the Mesa. Find her there inside the book.
Write numbers down. Don't call . . .

Taos, New Mexico—Napa California, 1998

NEAR THE CATHEDRAL

I used to get men mad so they would hit me.
Now I ask, she said. Sweating in that small room,
two blocks off Jackson Square. How brave
and honest he thought then. Foolish as they were.

New Orleans, Mardi Gras, 1973

ANNUNCIATION

I have bad news
the doctor said:

You've got
prostate cancer
and it's not
the good kind.

And I thought:
What is good cancer
anyway?

Cancer that lines up
in neat rows
turns homework in
on time
drops by for dinner
but takes the hint
to leave

and doesn't slouch
against the prostate
graffiti the seminal vesicles
or joy ride
to the colon
spine and brain?

But I didn't
make any jokes.

Didn't even say:
You'll never have to
numb me
next biopsy.

I can't feel a thing.

WAITING FOR THE OBVIOUS

The cowboy's Winchester is broken,
his horse's side raked by claws
of the grizzly the cowboy finally killed.

Two more grizzlies charge across
the ravine. The painting is about
what's not in the painting

yet—like all those Farside panels:
Santa's leg, for instance, dangling
out of the chimney, and sniffing

Santa's shoe, a huge Doberman.
But the painting's not funny,
nor my favorite Charlie Russell

work. I like his handmade postcards best
or the pictures that decorated letters
sent back to his Montana friends—

one of a woman on a scaffold with shaved
head—a serious matron examining her scalp:
Charlie's way of making fun

of the California border checks for insects
in foreign fruit they held even eighty
years ago, and still sometimes perform,

I've been stopped rolling in from Arizona
and asked about produce in my car.
But never searched. No one seems to care.

They've got better worries. Besides the border's
more in the air now than on the road. Approaching
that new border, they stop me or you

move electricity over our arms and thighs
examine our shoes for fuses,
searching for what comes next.

Los Angeles, 2002

TRANSFORMATION

Since she broke her hip
her face has become unfocused,
as if there's no point in what she sees.

She liked the pork chops,

tells me so a dozen times.
She takes my arm. Holds tight.
I'm a good son-in-law.

She thinks I'm strong.

for Jane, Ontario, 2004

CLOSURE

That summer after my father died
I spent the time at the swimming pool
killing flies, with my hands.
It's not hard. You spread your hands
wide apart with the fly in the center
then slap them together. Usually
the fly can't decide which way to go,
and there's a stain of blood and mucus
on each palm. Some days I got a hundred
though I'm not fast and wasn't then.
It's easy. Really. Anyone could learn.

Denver, 1958

REVISION

December 20, 2007

Twenty-one years ago
our house burned.
You rushed into my arms.

Cold morning,
stranger next to me.
Does kindling mourn

for when it was a tree?
Does darkness ache
becoming light?

for Ellen Williams 1946-2006

ON INDIRECTION AND RESTRAINT

That summer twilight was hide and seek.
And I was slow. Rarely made home
untagged. Even hiding inside the junipers,
covering myself with the itch of green,
edging my body next to the stucco wall.
But once I discovered a shed for garbage cans,
and stepped quickly in the scent of bad
meat, melon rinds—dull, blue buzz of flies.
Then I pulled the thick door carefully shut.
No one found me there or called. I waited
inside, motionless, day turning dark.

Denver, 1952

SURPRISE

When they entered her room
with its high four poster bed,
she turned her grandchildren's faces
down on the bureau, unwound
her silk wrap, warning:

there's a loaded gun between
the mattress and the wall. No
safety. He never hesitated at all.

Montclair, California, 2008

COYOTE CANYON

Past the turnoff
to the Alcoholic Trail
and a deep water crossing
that could drown a car
he comes to a half-mile
slope of boulders
he stopped at for years
watching other vehicles
struggle with the rocks.
He climbs in the new Jeep,
carefully putting tires,
on the bigger boulders.
Grace touching his arm.
At the top a wide plateau:
purple, yellow flowers.
willows where Anza
probably prayed. Not
too difficult. Almost spring.
Nothing here a metaphor

March 14, 2009, Anza Borrego

GRATITUDE

My Jeep did not slide off
the soaked freeway

No cell phone's tune
or daughter's plane
flaming out of sight

And I just got to watch
the *Agape Exterminators'* truck
roll down the street

with that Greek word
and fish symbol
painted on its side.

Yahweh is in anger management.
Godzilla is penned in Tokyo.
King Kong bats a giant tire
across a giant cage

Some of what I've said
is true.

November, 2005

A GRACE

Mist, cold rain outside
I pull on a soft sweater, think
of your mouth, skin, hands

for G., San Dimas, 2008

LUCKY

The funeral society that burned Mother
then cooled her in the Pacific, paid me
two thousand dollars because they mixed
her fire and ash with other fire and ash.
As if this mixture wasn't what we need.

1999

III:
THE MOJAVE ROAD AT LAST

LIVING ALONE AND ALMOST LIKING IT

The same room, mountains, dead grass outside,
clothes a carpet on the floor. Your pictures, ashes
on the shelf, I hardly look there now. I consider
women in supermarkets or displayed in magazines.
Sometimes I cook myself a meal. Wash my clothes
and dishes. Even watch TV. I don't need more
poems, scattered through the hard drive, filling the filing
cabinet, dropping from the desk. I should gather the old
ones together, arrange them into something new.

INTELLIGENT DESIGN

Consider the dodo, the swollen appendix,
small limbs under blubber in a whale.
All those strip malls of bone and hunger:
failed restaurants with for rent signs
pasted on cracked glass. Down my block
they ripped a filling station out, dug
up tanks for regular, diesel, and other
grades I've never used, bulldozed dirt
back into the hole. Three years of weeds
behind a chain link fence. Finally
a new station, with blue not yellow
logos on the pumps. I tell students:
save good lines from bad poems. Burros
in Death Valley, buffalo on Catalina,
kudzu choking bayous, feral swine
everywhere. Something will emerge.

WIDOWER'S AMBITION

He'd like to try other women
and find that they don't help.

NOT THE BEGINNING OF ANY FILM

1

Writing about
dead Ellen
he types my life
instead of wife.

2

When he was twelve
he thought euthanasia
was a student
exchange program
and wondered how
he might apply.
The counselor
they sent him to
didn't know either.

3

The widower
kicks his shoe off.
It wedges beneath
the brake pedal.
The Jeep crumbles
the Lexus.
Inside two widows,
one of them
is hurt.

CONTINUITY

Some in the bereavement group
sense their recent dead near:
a thud in the back bedroom
an almost stroke on the shoulder
a kiss that's not quite a kiss.

One woman's son appears
in white. He's happy where
he lives and doesn't live. They don't
make fun of him for being fat. Ellen
makes no visits. Gives no advice
about the woman that she saw
in her home, not even the playful pinch
she promised him whenever
a substitute came by. Then

Early morning. Twenty-fifth
Anniversary. Gaviota. Shelled
by the Japanese. Where
the new married couple
camped before Ellen helped
pedal their tandem up the pass.
How much she must have loved
him then. On a whim
he sleeps in the campground.

Stars. Only a good new bag
and a thin pad. The wind shakes
the camp. Most tents collapse.
He's warm but the ground
is sand and rock. He struggles out
to piss. Wraps up again. The wind
becomes a roar. He dreams
and Ellen's there. "Stop whining,"
she tells him, "about your back and feet."

"If that's how you feel," he says, repeating
an old fight, "any time you want to end
our relationship, is just fine with me."
Moon sheen on the ocean. Wind damps
its screams. Ten years ago he didn't mean
such words. Who knows what he means now?

April 9, 2007

A PROSE POEM THAT DOESN'T MENTION JEEPS

"The most important things are the hardest things to say."
—David St. John

What does he tell women about his obsession with the openings of
a blouse? How he's teenager crazy at more than sixty-six? How he
knows he's politically incorrect to the life lines in his hands, and, yes,
how he always peeks? Does he blame prostate cancer? His oncologist
stopped testosterone and gave him sadness, weight gain, hot flashes
in the night. When he complained, she told him, "Welcome to our
world." His wife, through lymphoma, laughed along. Is it some credit
that he thought, "How will I take care of my wife?" when he heard his
own bad cancer news? Should he mention a surprising gentleness, and
relief at not being led all places by his dick and never being tempted
to unfaithfulness? Is it only bragging to say he stopped the hormone
therapy to have energy for Ellen's final weeks? Will women be glad the
cancer's dormant, while the testosterone seeps back? Should he admit
that touching a woman's breast after four years, he felt something he
can't name? Can women tell he falls in love when one of them smiles
at him? Do they sense he might shatter if she held him naked through
the night? Muse, let him not seem foolish, sad, repellent. Could
women use him without pity? Should he dare a show of hands?

HOW IT IS

Words don't like me anymore.
And I don't like them.
They want to be in a book.
I want to revise my Jeep.
Give her a vocabulary of traction
an articulation of wheels.

My old words I give
to my daughter
for her U.C. applications
or my son for his thesis
on James Wright.
Neither of them drives
my Jeep.

I skip poetry for Jeep catalogues.
Learn the dialect they use:
locking and slip differentials,
suspension and body lifts
floating axles, sway bar
disconnects, skid plates,
rock sliders, winches, snatch blocks,
sand anchors, on-board air.

I want to guide my Jeep
up some hard desert road
nearly no one knows.
See the print of Beal's camels,
the track of Patton's tanks,
petroglyphs, soldiers'
graffiti , Willie Boy's
near forgotten grave.

Translate this sparse language.
Give you different words.

CHI

He can't understand
her love.
Not the damp
thrust and moan
of fucking.

But how
she can move
her hands over
his clothed arm
and chest

until he's not
his name
then hold
one hand above
his pant leg
and will
a wave of heat.

for P.

THE MOJAVE ROAD AT LAST

started in sand and rocks
near the parking lot and slot
machines of Avi Casino,
speedboats churning the river.
A day later, after the Dead Mountains
and the notch of Piute Pass,
Lanfair Valley and the New York Peaks
were thick with cholla and Joshua—
a sharpened forest denser
than the famous one
miles south. How many see
Lanfair's trees? A few.

Crossing Dry Soda Lake
which wasn't dry, nor wet enough
to stick Jeeps there, our group reached
the monument in the center. Each
tossed a rock, as travelers do,
on the surrounding pile and scanned
words on the brass plaque—no
I won't tell you what they said.

BLESSING

Back from the Mojave Road. He
dreamed next to a new woman.
He was walking with his first lover,
who changed to his dead wife.
Something was not between them,
and he asked if she still loved
him. She said, "No" calmly
as if it were "Yes," or the directions
to a house. Nothing hurt. She
moved upward and ahead. Suddenly
she was naked and more than
beautiful. Then the threads of light
that were Ellen unknit. And
each thread went its own way.

NOTES

AFTER VISITING HIS UROLOGIST, HE THINKS OF THE MOJAVE ROAD

For a mile-by-mile description of the Mojave Road and its history, see Dennis Casebier, *Mojave Road Guide*. Goffs Schoolhouse: Tales of the Mojave Road Publishing, 1999.

Lowering tire pressure to 10 or 15 pounds is a way of maintaining traction in sand and mud. For off-road technique, as well as a briefer description of the Mojave Road, and other rides, see Peter Massey and Jeanne Wilson, *Backcountry Adventures Southern California*. Castle Rock, Colorado: Swagman Publishers.

DISCUSSING THE MOJAVE ROAD WITH ODYSSEUS

Most of the gear mentioned here and elsewhere are modifications for stock vehicles for maintaining traction and clearance off-road. The winch is for when these things don't work. See Backcountry Adventures above, Moses Ludel, *Jeepowners Bible*. Cambridge: Bentley, 2004 or almost any guide to four-wheeling.

JORDAN

The ruins of Jordan are just off California 395. Bodie was one of the last California gold rush towns and a notoriously rough place. "Goodbye God. I'm going to Bodie," said one traveler. It is now a well-preserved ghost town, over twenty miles northeast of Jordan. See Roger Mitchell, *High Sierra SUV Trails, volume 1*. Oakhurst California: Track and Trail, 2002. Some of the accounts of Jordon vary slightly. The rescue party may have come on snowshoes, in addition to skis, but I prefer skis. Elsewhere in these poems I have made choices. Undoubtedly I have also made factual mistakes.

HOW IT IS

Most of the terms here describe equipment for serious four-wheeling where traction and clearance are issues. The rest are for "self-recovery"—getting out of trouble on one's own. A "sand anchor," for instance, is a device for using a winch when trapped and alone in deep sand, or even snow. Perhaps everyone should have a sand anchor near.

"Lessons" and "Gift" appeared in *O'Brien Literary Speculator;* "Perspective" was published in *The American Indian Culture and Research Journal* of U.C.L.A.; and "Homily" and "Closure" appeared in *Beyond the Valley of the Contemporary Poets.*

Many of the other poems first appeared in the chapbooks *The Mojave Road at Last* (Conflux Press) and in *Stratification* (Inevitable Press).

This book was set in 11.5 point Baskerville